HARRY IS G

A Hide-and-Seek Story

Written by Sarah Reid Chisholm
Illustrated by Michelle Neavill

Augsburg
MINNEAPOLIS

HAMSTER FOOD

HARRY IS GONE!
A Hide-and-Seek Story

Scripture is taken from the Holy Bible, New International Version, copyright © 1973, 1978, 1984 by the International Bible Society. Used by permission of Zondervan Bible Publishers.

    ISBN 0-8066-2741-7   LCCN 94-72212

Manufactured in the U.S.A.   AF 9-2741

98 97 96 95 94 1 2 3 4 5 6 7 8 9 10

For my parents,
who let me have a hamster
and a guinea pig
but not a rat
S.R.C.

For my sisters,
Lori, Patty, and Janine
M.L.N.

*Cast all your anxiety on him because he
cares for you.*
—1 Peter 5:7 NIV

Saturday started out great. I watched cartoons, shot some hoops and played with my cars.

Then I saw Harry's cage.
"Harry is gone!" I shrieked.

I looked in my closet

. . . and crawled under my bed.

I searched behind my desk and in my toy box. No Harry.

Now what would I do? My parents had promised to buy me a pet snake if I took really good care of Harry. I had to find Harry before my parents knew he was missing.

I sprinkled hamster food around the room and placed celery in a shoe box near the door. I waited . . . and I waited . . . and I waited. Harry didn't show up.

So I decided to search
every room of the house
inch by inch. First I
looked in the hallway . . .

then in the bathroom.

My sister made me wait
outside while she searched
her room.

Then I went downstairs. Mom and Dad were busy getting ready to give a big party.

"I'm trying to find one of my cars,"
I said.

I wanted to tell them the truth so they could help me find Harry. But I was afraid I might get in trouble.

It was getting late, and the doorbell started ringing . . . *brring, brring, brring.* People were coming for the party.

I kept searching.

I watched for Harry near plates of food. (Harry likes to eat!)

I looked in ladies' purses.
No Harry. I was starting
to feel really, really bad.

It was time to tell my parents.

"I can't talk now,"
my mother told me.

"Later," said my dad,
when I tapped him
on the shoulder.

I missed Harry. He was my best buddy when things went wrong. He'd climb in my pocket and squirm around 'til he was comfortable. Then he'd stick his head out and just stare at me. I could talk to Harry about anything. What would I do without him?

Late that night, after everyone went home, I crept downstairs. Mom had gone to bed. I told Dad about Harry. He looked a little angry at first.

Then he said, "Hamsters like to play at night. Let's wait for Harry and see if he comes out."

We sat together on the couch.

"God cares about Harry," said my dad.

"How do you know?" I asked.

"Jesus said that God knows when a sparrow falls to the ground. A sparrow is a very small bird, even smaller than Harry. I'm sure God knows where Harry is. He also cares very much about a little boy who is sad. Why don't you ask God to help you find Harry?"

So I prayed for Harry. Then we both fell asleep.

Early in the morning, I blinked open my eyes. Mom was standing right in front of me. I couldn't believe what I saw. Harry sat in her hands nibbling on a piece of celery.

"Did you know Harry had escaped from his cage?" she asked me. "I found him in the kitchen this morning."

I grabbed Harry and hugged him.
"Thank you, Lord," I whispered.

Then I told my parents, "I lied about
losing one of my cars. I was really
looking for Harry. He has been missing since
yesterday morning. I wish I'd told you
both sooner."

Harry brushed his whiskers against my cheek, climbed on my shoulder and into my pocket. He squirmed around 'til he was comfortable, stuck his head out and just stared at me.

My parents aren't ready for me to have a snake yet. That's O.K. I'm just glad Harry is back.

THE END